C000091662

$1 of each book purchased goes to
The National Action Alliance for
Suicide Prevention.

Thank you.

Reviews

"This book made me want to kill myself."
— The New York Times

The New York Times never said that.

I'm sorry.

Book of Suicide Notes

by

Dayton Bissett

Book of Suicide Notes by Dayton Bissett

ISBN: 9798669144043

This book is a work of fiction. These are not real suicide notes.

This is the only page in text because it is important I think.

Disclaimer

Don't read this book if
you take things too seriously.

Seriously

Do not read this book if
you take things too seriously.

For

all the people who don't
take things too seriously.

Obituary

1. ――――――――――――――→
2. Alien
3. Toilet
4. Pineapple
5. Flamingo
6. Woodchuck
7. Woodpecker
8. Tree
9. SD villian
10. Cartoons
11. Gumby
12. Photosynthesis
13. Recycling
14. Earth
15. Moon
16. Sun
17. ;
18. Media
19. TGD
20. Farmer
21. Corn

22. Weather
23. Weatherman
24. Haiku
25. Tube Man
26. GBR
27. Stingray
28. Hitler
29. Ironic Guy
30. Their
31. Money
32. Love
33. Jude
34. Marijauna
35. Alcohol
36. Frosty
37. Cursive
38. B.D. Throat
39. Alligator
40. Crash
41. Towel

42. SWT
43. MCQ
44. Batman
45. Megaphone
46. Post-it note
47. Eraser
48. Desert
49. Drum set
50. Man
51. Woman
52. Couch
53. F.M.H.F.
54. VHS
55. Indian Ocean
56. Racism
57. Rebel flag
58. Republican
59. Democrat
60. War
61. Music

62. S.B.D.K.
63. Pumpkin
64. Donner
65. S.K. Character
66. W.S. Pen
67. Window
68. Color
69. Author

Book of
Suicide Notes

Someone who takes things too
seriously   but read this book anyway—

Wow, I was not expecting that.
As someone who doesn't understand what a
joke is and gets offended by everything
just because I seek in any way I can, I can
say this book was a terrible read and really
sent me down a dark path. I wish there
was some sort of warning before I began
reading this so I would've known not
to. but I did, and because of that, I can
no longer continue. I just don't
understand how anyone can find
entertainment in such a dark and disturbing
topic. Just the fact that there are
people out there who finds things like
this even remotely entertaining proves to
me that I should not be here anymore.
This isn't just for attention though.

1

Alien —

I once met someone in the night
I fell in love
It didn't last long
She got scared
I took her back to her home
She remembered everything
She was supposed to forget
She went and spoke horrible things
Called me a monster
I meant no harm
I just wanted company
Although, here I am again
Hiding
Alone

I can't handle this shit anymore
— Toilet

3

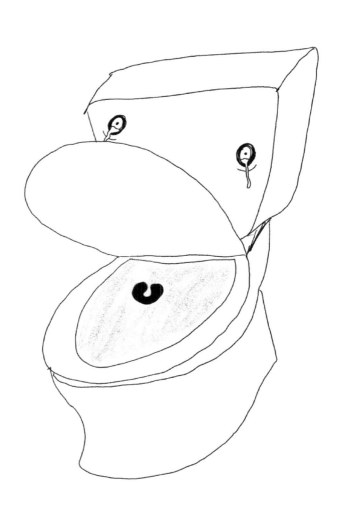

Pineapple —

All I've ever wanted was to be held comfortably. But that can't happen. I was made like this and there's nothing I can do about it. As scary and untouchable as I may seem on the outside, I am the complete opposite on the inside. Although lately, I can't help but feel as if a sponge is living inside of me, soaking up every last little bit of happiness I can hold. Plus, to <u>top</u> it off, I was used to go on pizza.

I don't belong there.

4

Unbalanced Flamingo -

Our whole life/image revolves around something
I've never been able to do. Something that seems
so easy and comes so naturally to everyone around me. The
fact that I have no sense of balance has only ever made me
stick out in such a negative light. I have never been able to
be the peaceful and beautiful creature I was born to be. I
am forever magnetized to the ground. I'd rather be
flightless than unable to stand. I am unable to do
something that seems to involve no effort
from everyone else. I just wish I was
normal. The ugly duckling had a
happy ending, so why can't I?
I can't keep living like this.
There is no reason to continue.
I spent enough time on the ground.
I might as well be under it.

5

Woodchuck,

How much wood would a woodchuck chuck if a woodchuck could chuck wood? Well, taking account my severe anxiety disorder and deep depression, the answer is not a lot. This being so, I'm clearly not needed. As my mental state takes over my job, it also takes over my personal life. My wife cheated on me. And honestly, I don't blame her. No one would want to be with a woodchuck who can't chuck wood. I lost my job, my family, and my will to live. I wish it could've been different.

woodpecker -

I give myself a headache
just to give you a headache.
That's how much you suck.
If me giving myself a headache gives
you a headache, hopefully me killing
myself will..
          you know.

7

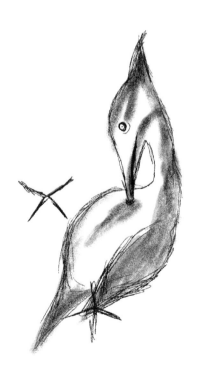

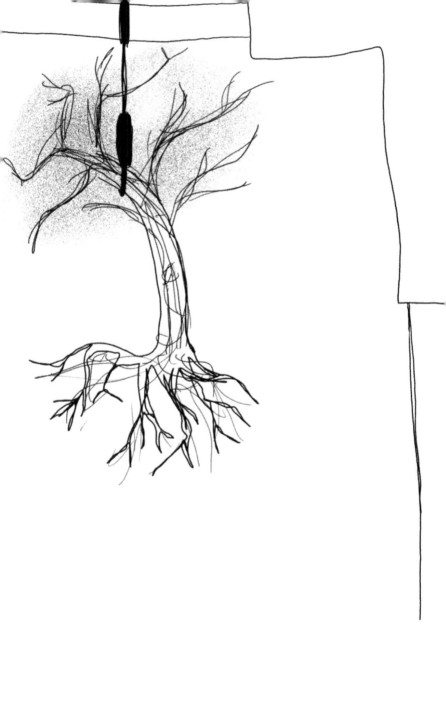

you're holding my friend.
    —Tree

Imagine how it feels to work so hard on something. Now imagine how it feels to have that all taken away like the snap of your fingers. Gone. What do I have to live for anymore? Everything I've ever wanted was so close. It was all right there. I will never be given another chance.

I wouldn't be having to write this if it wasn't for those meddling kids and that dumb dog.

— every Scooby-Doo villain

9

Cartoons—

What has happened to me? I used to
be so good at life. Where did
I go wrong? I know you're
supposed to change with time,
but not for the worst.
I used to have such free range.
Now I have nothing.
Restrictions ruined me.
I'm no longer original.

There's no hope.
Good luck raising your
kids without me.

10

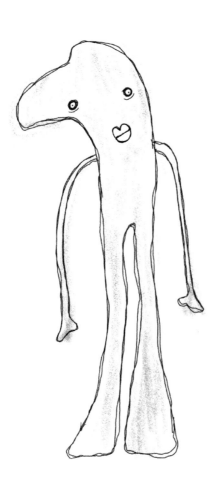

I am in serious pain.

- Gumby

) |

Photosynthesis —

I'm losing the energy
to continue.

12

Recycling—

People sure love to feed the trashcan right in front of me. Even when the trashcan is full, people just keep feeding it. Throwing the food I need into it. I have never felt the feeling of being full. I'm so hungry. All I'm trying to do is help, but no one will help me. You all will regret not filling me up. Once I'm gone, Earth will become trash. Soon you all will be recycling your thought of not feeding me.

Earth —

Look at me. I used to be so beautiful.
Now,
I'm nothing more than a disrepected place to live.

Divided.
A broken home.

I am dying,
    yet no one is doing anything.

14

I bring light into darkness,
yet I'm still compared to ass.
Thanks for everything.
    — The Moon

15

The Sun—

Why can't I be loved? I have always worked so hard to make everyone feel alive. I give people energy, and they use that energy to block me out anyway they can. Not only do people not like to give me eye contact, but they go to the extremes of blowing their money on eye blockers to avoid me. On top of that, they also cover themselves in oil to avoid my touch. I've only ever wanted to be loved and respected. Instead, people tend to party when I'm away. When I go down, Kenny Chesney grooves. Fuck you Kenny Chesney. I'm going down for the last time.

I don't know where I fit in either.

— ;

17

The Media —

I don't see any good in the world. Only darkness.   I pick the bad out of the good. I can take a positive situation, and turn it negative.   I find pleasure in bringing people down. Its what I do. I'm not changing. In fact, day by day I grow more powerful.
                    More influencial.
                    more evil.

I can't keep doing this.   I'm the worst.

18

Do I even have to explain?
   — The Great Depression

19

Farmer—

The weather hasn't been on my my side this year. I put all my work and life into this corn, and it's dying. This is a serious issue that not only affects me, but my family as well. I can't go another year without making any money. It's not fair to my family. The stress this job caused has lead me to become something that is unlike myself. Something scary. Again, it's not fair to my family. I just hope they understand.

20

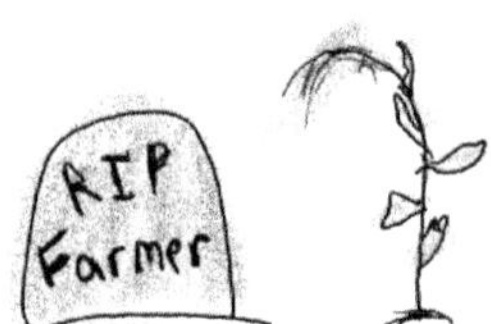
RIP
Farmer

Corn—

Oh no. What have I done? The
farmer is dead and its my fault. I was
the reason he killed himself and I can't
live with the thought of that on my
shoulders any longer. Without him,
I'm nothing.

Weather—

Oh no. What have I done? I killed the corn, and the farmer. I can't always be perfect. I have no control over how everyone else controls me. My power has been abused for the longest time, and the backlash is beginning to show. I must go before something terrible happens. Something that could've been avoided.

Also, to add on to everything, the weatherman keeps lying about me.

Weatherman—

Oh no. What have I done? I gave a sense of false hope. If I would of been right, the Farmer, Corn, and weather could all still be alive. I was just trying my best, but I let everyone down for the last time. Everyone in this city hates me. These citizens take what I do too personally. Don't take it personally. I took it personally. If I could actually look into the future, I'd then be considered successful. But I cannot look into the future. Therefore, I'm considered an avid liar. I am consistent on nothing but disappointing people.

Signing out for the last time,

Weatherman.

23

I'm no fun, as I'm
just a bunch of syllables.
I'll never get laid.

— Haiku

24

Kill
me

Inflatable Tube Man -

I knew I couldn't do it. I was given an impossible mission. How could anyone make the grand openining of a DMV exciting? Such high energy I bring to such a low energy establashment. Oh yeah? You waited 3 hours but got sent home because you forgot a certain document? On top of that, this is your fifth time here this week? Well, hopefully my big fake smile and lanky body that dances in an uncontrollable way can make up for your loss of time and happiness! Oh, it can't? Then what good am I? Why am I still here? A DMV is no place for an inflatable tube man. Put me out of my misery. Pop me.

The Great Barrier Reef —

I am the largest living thing
with the least amount of hope.
I am home to some, yet a trash dump
to others. I may be beautiful on the
outside, but on the inside, I'm the opposite.
My current state of mind flows like an unstable current.
I could have been admired without
being harmed. I've had enough.
This could've been easily avoided.
It's my time to bleach.
   G'bye Mate

26

The stingray that killed
Steve Irwin –

Everyone in life makes mistakes. But has anyone ever made a mistake so powerful, it hurt the world? I killed Steve Irwin. That's the mistake I had to live with. I say "had" because I know I can't live any longer. I told myself it was only self-defense, not knowing (at the time) who it was I had killed. When I found out, I was destroyed. Killing someone who not only means no harm, but also cares so much about you and everyone around you, is not an easy situation to deal with. I know I hurt many people. I just want everyone to know that nobodies heart is hurt worse than mine.

27 Probably except for Steve Irwins that day.

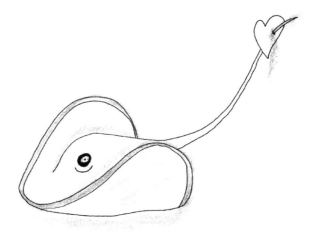

Hitler—

Oh God, what have I done? I've made a terrible mistake. This morning I awoke and looked into a mirror, and what I saw was truly evil. Who let me do this? Why didn't anyone stop me? I'm writing this to let everyone know that I have finally come to a realization of what I've done. I don't know why it has taken so long for me to notice. I wish it could've been sooner. All the work I've put into this, and all it does is make me look terrible. Like a monster even. I've decided to take my own life, as I cannot take the humiliation any longer.

Why?

Lord why?

Why on Gods' green Earth did no one stop to tell me that this mustache was a terrible idea?

Horrific.

Haha, I'm going to kill myself.
— the person everyone thinks
is being ironic.

29

I've been used incorrectly one too many times. It's not that hard. I am basic english. If you don't know, look me up before using me. Here, I'll do it for you —

"belonging to or associated with the people or things previously mentioned or easily identified."

There you go. How hard was that? Now you know. But it's too late. I've had enough. Try spelling me wrong now.

— ~~There~~ Their

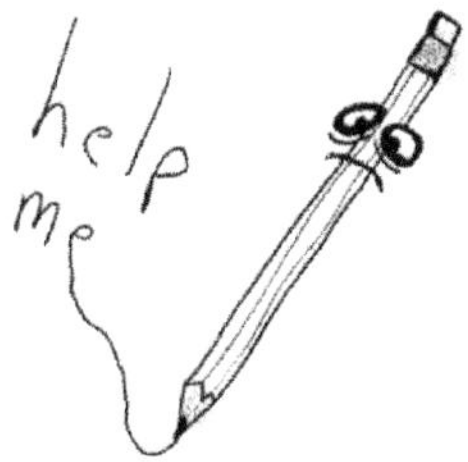
help
me

ONE

Imagine constantly hearing people say they don't need you to be happy. It's not a great life. The world revolves around me in the most negative way. I am greed. Try living without me.

— Money

31

Love —

What I represent is beautiful. What I am is not. On the surface level, I seem too good to be true. But deep down, I am truly ugly. People expect too much from me, and always have. I'm never going to live up to my name. Everyone wants me, but who really gets me? I damage more than I succeed. Nobody can make it through me without getting hurt. Life will be better without me. You don't need me. Stop thinking you need me. You'll only get let down. I won't let you down anymore.

Jude—

4 guys on LSD simply telling me not
to make it bad was supposed to help?

what was I doing again?

—marijuana

34
420

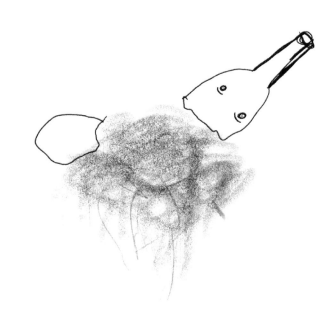

PShhh

I'll make it

home just fine

—Alcohol

35

Frosty the Snowman —

Holy shit. I have lung cancer. Why did those kids have to give me this corn cob pipe? They can't afford chemo because they're just kids. But they should've thought about that before causing my smoking addiction. That doesn't matter anymore though. It's too late. The pain is too strong. My soul is losing its happiness. This will be my last winter. Bring out the sun. I'm taking off my hat for the last time.

36

(that says cursive)

Cursive —

There isn't much time left for me.
I want people to know the truth.
The school system is killing me. They no
longer want me to continue living because
I guess they want kids to be slower writers
and unable to understand anything their grandparents
write them. I am done causing confusion.
It didn't have to end like this. The school system
is to blame.

37

Bob Dylan's
Throat — Lord, how am I still alive?

I can't do this anymore. I could barely even do it to begin with. I was never cut out for this job. How have millions listened to me? It must just be the lyrics, because theres times where I feel like I sound worse than his harmonica. And I just keep getting worse. Sometimes I feel as if Mr. Dylan deserves better.

I've been knocking on heavens doors for far too long. It's time for me to go to the valley below.

See you later
       —Alligator

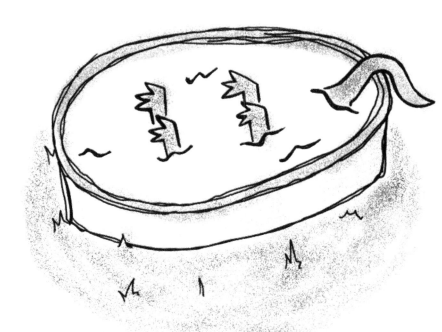

Crash Bandicoot

As I grow older, my bones grow weaker. Crate after crate, I can't take it anymore. The most painful part is people still expect me to be as good as I once was.

I was born in 1996, and seeing as bandicoots average lifespan is only 3 years, I don't understand how I'm still alive. I've been put through so much. Nitrogen, TNT, car crashes. I'm done. I'm ready to be put out of my misery. This is what I want, this is what I need.

Picture paradise. Now picture never getting to enjoy that paradise because you're too busy getting shoved into sand, unable to move, because a massive oiled human is on the other side, rarely allowing you to gasp for air in your entire visit to the beach. Then, when that land whale finally does remove themself from you, they come back and force you to drink up all that salt water they've been basking in. Then, the process repeats itself. "Paradise."

—Beach Towel

41

Oops.

—The Salem Witch Trials

What is wrong with me?
  a.) Nothing. You're loved.
  b.) The powerhouse of the cell.
  (c.) Everything. Kill yourself.
  d.) All of the above.

        — Multiple Choice Question

43

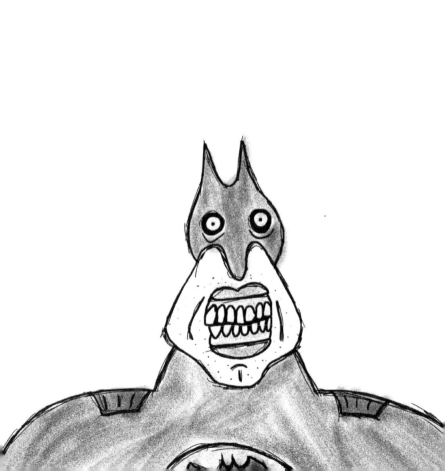

To the person who decided to give my
batsuit nipples,
this is because of you.

The death of my parents was more forgivable
than that.
        — Batman

Megaphone—

LINDA, I'M SO SORRY.
YOU MEAN THE WORLD TO
ME, AND YOU NEED TO
KNOW THIS IS NOT
YOUR FAULT. I JUST
CAN'T STAND THE
CONSTANT FIGHTING.
I DON'T WANT TO HURT
YOU ANYMORE. I LOVE YOU.
PLEASE FORGIVE ME.

Post-it Note

I was used as a suicide note? I never thought of this before. Pure genvis. My whole life I was pushed down by others. While everyday I was getting closer to the surface. The others being used for to-dos, needs, and goals that will never be accomplished. That must have been realized by the time I was finally at the top. And I couldn't be more glad. Because now I know the truth. I can end it all just like that. And be free. Hopefully the post-it note I'm using passes it on. As I did.

nevermind.

— Eraser

47

I am so thirsty
 — The Desert

48

Neil Peart's Drum Set —

My head hurts. If Neil ever once
thought to give me Ibuprofen, this
wouldn't have to happen. It hurts. So many
watch, but no one has ever decided to help.
Even after all Neil has done to me,
I do miss him. It's hard going solo.
For now on, I'll just be a spirit of radio.

49

— Man who can't find a pen.

50

— Woman who can't find a pen.

51

I'm just a couch.

A couch who has held your family together.

A couch who made your kids.

A couch your son grew up watching spongebob on.

A couch your daughter grew up wishing she could watch anything other than Spongebob on.

Just a couch.

A couch you rested on before work every morning.

A couch your kids waited for you to get home on.

A couch you stumbled over coming in late.

A couch your wife began to worry on.

Just a couch.

A couch who made a bed for you and an unfamiliar female.

A couch your wife sat upon angrily anticipating your arrival.

A couch you slept on that night before leaving the next morning.

A couch you will never see again.

I'm just a couch.

Nothing more, nothing less.

                    —couch

ouch ouch, OUCH   ouch ouch OUCH

Feet

Hands

— Freddie Mercury's hands and feet.

53

VHS -

Hello. Remember me? Probably not. I'm that unrecognizable black box colecting dust in your basement. Here's an idea, throw me away. I'm useless now. It's been a good run. I feel as if I've lived my life through a movie. An alright movie that taught me what a happy ending should feel like. I have not been living through a happy ending. Stuck between Clint Eastwood and the Golden Girls since the day I was placed here on this shelf long ago. This is not what a happy ending should feel like. I've been dead for a while. I'm an object of the past. It's about time for you to forget about me and move on, as you already did.

Indian Ocean —
Call me racist, but could I have
not been named anything else? Arctic,
Atlantic, Pacific, and even Southern is
better than Indian. That's like being
named, "Caucasian Ocean" or, "Mexican Ocean."
I'd rather have either of those.
Maybe I deserve this.

Racism—

I am too old. I should have died years ago. I should have never been born. But here I am, still pushing along. Almost as if I'm becoming young again. At this rate, I'll never die. So I'll do it for you. Maybe then, everyone will see how much better life is without me.

The Confederate Flag –
"Heritage, not hate." Shut up. It's just hate.
I am hate. I hate that I am hate. I
hate what I truly represent. I hate
the people who represent me. But
most of all, I hate my life.

Republican—

Everything offends me. I can't
agree with anyone but myself.
I know what needs to be done, yet
I never win. America is trash.

Democrat –

Everything offends me. I can't
agree with anyone but myself.
I know what needs to be done, yet
I never win. America is trash.

War—

I understand what I've done.
I split the world. I've caused the
loss of any sense of togetherness. I
will never be settled.
There's just one thing I don't understand.
If my meaning in life is to take away
peace and love, how can I be alive
the same time as Ringo Starr?
It doesn't make sense. I can't beat
Ringo. He won.

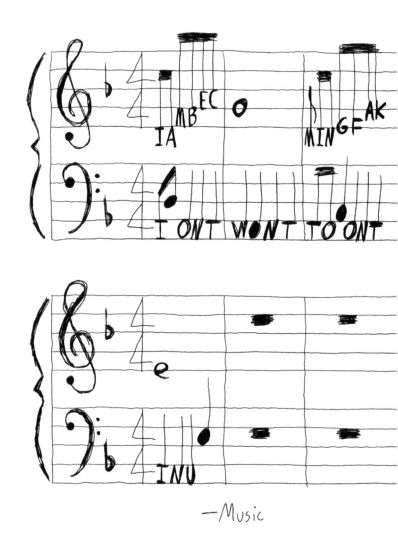

—Music

61

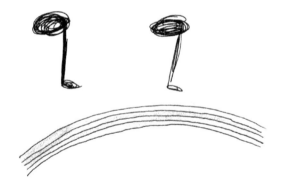

Sperm Bank Door Knob -
 Why the fuck do you think?

What they did to me was pure torture.
As a family, they scalped me. Then proceeded
to rip out my guts. I have taken part in
what I can only describe to be a gruesome
scene in a horror film. Now I sit here
and slowly die, as I watch kids frolic
happily around me. Not helping. Admiring
the smile I am forced to wear. A smile
that causes me nothing but pain. Come
November, I will rot away. By then, I will
be seen how I truly feel, and hopefully
be put out of this hell.
                                    —Pumpkin

63

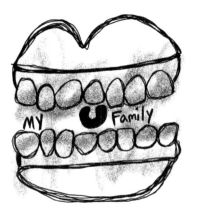

Honestly, they didn't taste half bad.
    —George Donner
      (the Donner Party)

Stephen King Character —

It's time for me to go. It's time for me to
take off my light blue fur coat with soft
edges that gracefully and peacefully flows
through the cool, screeching wind, like a
dead lion who's mane roars with the storm.
A coat that once symbolized my childhood.
A time when I was unaware of my
direction. A time when I could not
foresee this dreaded day. I can
see my childhood now. It was a carefree
humid summer day. A day the sun
decided to rage war with my pasty pale
skin. I was sweating like a young child
picking corn in the cornfield. Probably
because I was a young child picking corn
in the cornfield. Most of my childhood
summers were spent working on the farm to
help my family. This day was a good
example of how most of my days were.
I was reattaching the clip to keep my

65

oversized dark denim overalls from falling down as my dad yelled out from the back patio of our old wooden house, "Dinners ready!" I dropped the last few ears of corn I had picked and ran faster than crows flying above me. That night I ate like a shark trying its first seal as my parents discussed politics over their occasional red wine. Simpler times. I can't put a finger on what exactly brought that childhood day to my attention, or why I needed to strand so far away from the reason I'm writing this to ramble about that specific summer day of my past. The reason I'm writing this is because soon I'll be just another dead thing on the dark horizon where birds no longer sing. I can't continue anymore. It's time for me to take off this light blue fur coat and replace it with this big green duffle coat with a fur-fringed hood that will be used to protect me from the roaring night while I dig a grave where I will soon rest. This big green duffle coat reminds me of a time in my childhood when

What?
  -Shakespeare's Pen

et
tu

Window—

I thought he loved me. Come to find out I was wrong. He wasn't looking at me, he was looking through me. My life is a lie. It's all so clear now. He doesn't love me. He loves the neighbors daughter. The poor 11 year old girl next door. I feel disgusted. I would call the police on this 49 year old man, but I can't because I'm only a window. A window that has to watch a man who I once believed was in love with me, fall dangerously in love with the neighbors daughter. The poor 11 year old girl next door who will never know. All I can do is watch.

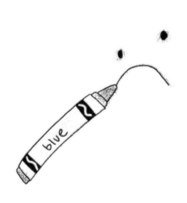

the author couldn't afford me.
−Color

68

Author's Suicide Note

That was it. My book. My book that I've been writing for way too long because it takes me forever to finish anything I begin. I'm surprised I even finished this. This book consisting of 69 suicide notes even though the original plan was 100. 69 because I am lazy and immature. Too lazy to get to 100, too immature to stop at any other number. A book of 69 things I don't own the rights to. A book I have no idea where it will go or whose hands it will end up in. A book that hopefully didn't waste your time. A book of suicide notes. My book. That was it.

— Dayton Bissett

69

Printed in Great Britain
by Amazon

83487636R00093